In reading the Little Lou story and looking at the life-like illustrations of this colorful adventure, I am at once taken back to a time and place . . . and a people . . . that I have known all of my life and that I have carried with me in all of my travels.

My songs and music are inspired by people like Little Lou and the neighborhood characters who frequent Cab's place . . . the neighborhood bar in the story.

Little Lou represents so many little black boys who grow up with a burning desire, and ample talent, to play the blues. Nurtured by the elder blues men in the family or in the neighborhood (which is usually an extended family) these youngsters attend the first and vast vital school of their future careers . . . schools with experienced instructors in the basic of music, the blues, in friendships and in a way of life bound together with pain, laughter, love and music.

Bluesingly yours,
Memphis Slim

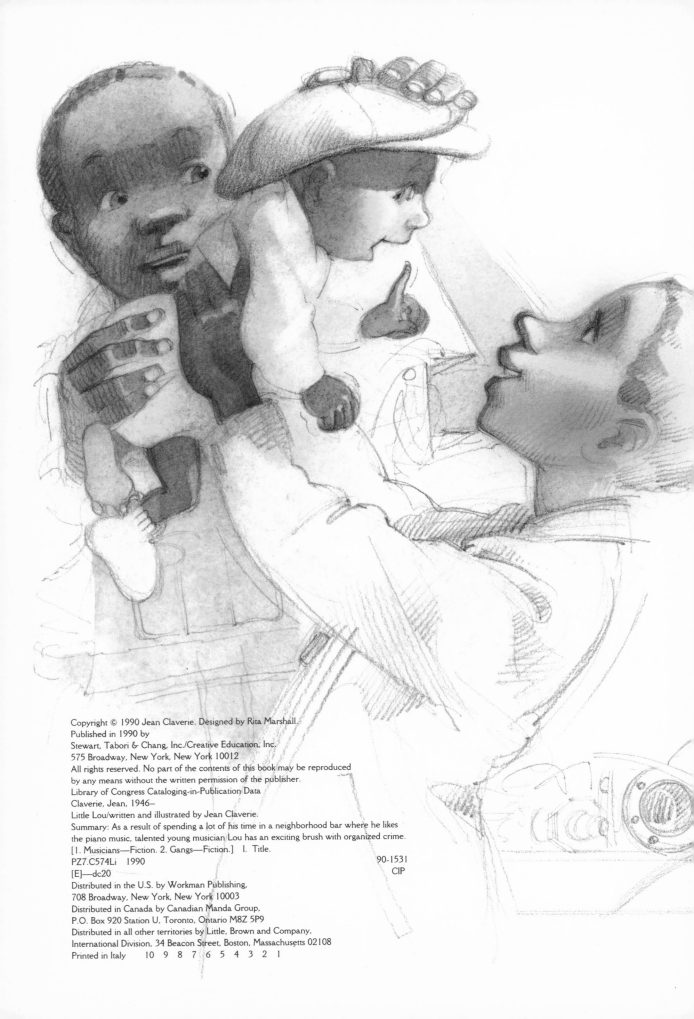

Copyright © 1990 Jean Claverie. Designed by Rita Marshall.
Published in 1990 by
Stewart, Tabori & Chang, Inc./Creative Education, Inc.
575 Broadway, New York, New York 10012
Library of Congress Cataloging-in-Publication Data
Claverie, Jean, 1946–
Little Lou/written and illustrated by Jean Claverie.
Summary: As a result of spending a lot of his time in a neighborhood bar where he likes
the piano music, talented young musician Lou has an exciting brush with organized crime.
[1. Musicians—Fiction. 2. Gangs—Fiction.] I. Title.
PZ7.C574Li   1990   90-1531
[E]—dc20   CIP
Distributed in the U.S. by Workman Publishing,
708 Broadway, New York, New York 10003
Distributed in Canada by Canadian Manda Group,
P.O. Box 920 Station U, Toronto, Ontario M8Z 5P9
Distributed in all other territories by Little, Brown and Company,
International Division, 34 Beacon Street, Boston, Massachusetts 02108
Printed in Italy   10 9 8 7 6 5 4 3 2 1

LITTLE LOU

BY JEAN CLAVERIE

STEWART, TABORI & CHANG
NEW YORK
CREATIVE EDUCATION INC.
MANKATO

Thanks to Buster Benton, Diane and Alice; Rob
Bowman, from the Center for Southern Folklore
(Memphis TN); Allan Eady, Tom and George
Peterson, Donald and Kathy Zepp, and Mem-
phis Slim, who will never see this story published
and to whom it is dedicated.

Momma says the blues started inside me way back before I was born, with my daddy and Uncle Sonny, but I got
my big break thanks to gangsters. It's a long story . . .

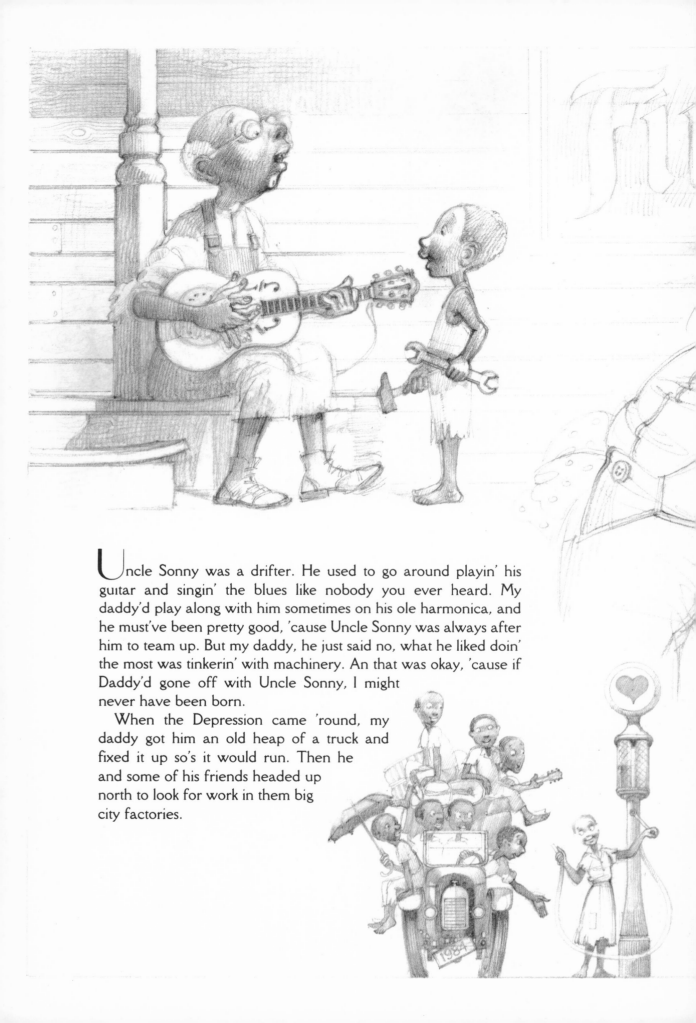

Uncle Sonny was a drifter. He used to go around playin' his guitar and singin' the blues like nobody you ever heard. My daddy'd play along with him sometimes on his ole harmonica, and he must've been pretty good, 'cause Uncle Sonny was always after him to team up. But my daddy, he just said no, what he liked doin' the most was tinkerin' with machinery. An that was okay, 'cause if Daddy'd gone off with Uncle Sonny, I might never have been born.

When the Depression came 'round, my daddy got him an old heap of a truck and fixed it up so's it would run. Then he and some of his friends headed up north to look for work in them big city factories.

Along the way, they had to stop for gas. That gal on the pumps must've taken a shine to my daddy, 'cause after the tank got filled, she climbed aboard and went off with 'em. One more didn't make no difference to that ole truck. That gal, she was Momma.

When they got to the city, they all started lookin' for work, but findin' a job just wasn't as easy as the folks back home had said. After a lotta lookin', my daddy found a place needin' a mechanic, and a couple of pay days later, he and my momma fixed themselves up with some fancy new clothes and went along to Reverend Pickett.

Momma and Daddy found a place to live up over a bar with a side door right into the garage where Daddy worked. On pay day, all the neighborhood folks would come over to the Bird Nest—that was the name of the bar—to dance and play cards and listen to Slim. Slim was always there on pay day.

Then, as the times got harder, there'd be more folks at the Bird Nest every night, dancin' their troubles away. Slim just about lived at that ole bar. It would get kinda hard for my momma and daddy to get any sleep, so they'd go on down and join the party. After a while, they got to know all the folks. My daddy says none of 'em was rich, but I bet none of 'em was downright miserable either, on account of Ole Slim and his piano.

Then I came along. Momma says I was a singer right from when I was born. She says I sang with the gramophone in the kitchen and I sang with the radio in the garage. Sometimes, I remember, my daddy'd pull out his ole harmonica and join in with me, if he wasn't too busy fixin' a carburetor or a clutch. It seems like we just had the music in our souls.

And, of course, we all sang in church.

"If God made man in His own image," Reverend Pickett used to say every Sunday, "it must surely be that the Good Lord is fond of music, too." Then away we'd go: "A-mazing Grace, how sweet the sound . . ."

Wasn't nobody ever missed out on church service.

Now Momma was real sure I had talent, and so it wasn't too long before she started me takin' music lessons with Miss Blandish. Miss Blandish lived uptown, where they had folks sweepin' the streets. I didn't much care for them lessons, but I guess it didn't hurt me none to learn about fellas like Bach and Grieg and Mozart.

But what I really liked doin' the most was goin' down to the Bird Nest each night before Momma called me for supper. Slim knew all the tunes my daddy said Uncle Sonny used to play, and some new stuff, too, that he fancied up a bit. And he'd always show me somethin' fine. But when he'd start in singin' the blues, I could feel 'em right down to my toes. I guess anybody could feel them blues when Slim was singin'.

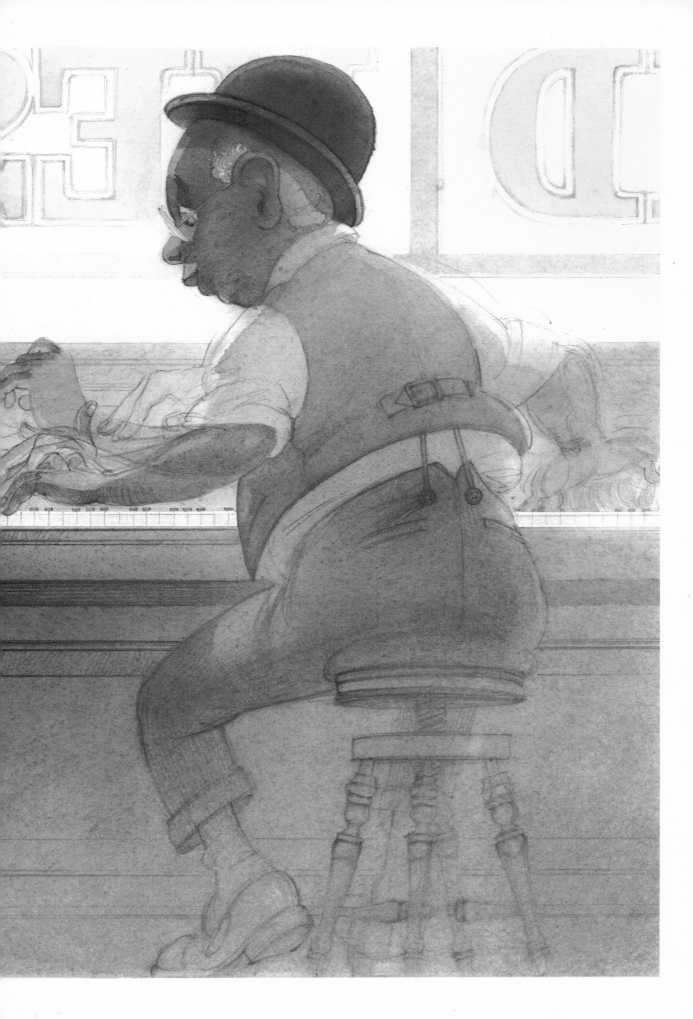

Then one night right in the middle of a tune, Slim just collapsed and he fell off that stool he'd been sittin' on for the past six years. The Doc came, but it was too late. The joy went out of the folks then, and out of me, too.

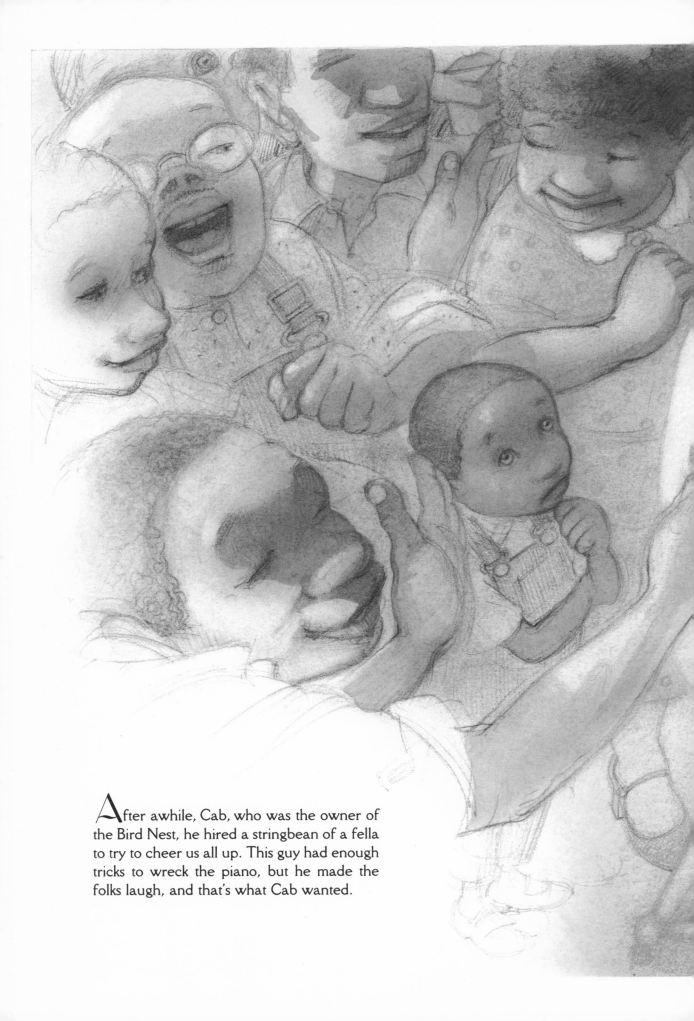

After awhile, Cab, who was the owner of the Bird Nest, he hired a stringbean of a fella to try to cheer us all up. This guy had enough tricks to wreck the piano, but he made the folks laugh, and that's what Cab wanted.

Then, when good times came back and things started lookin' up for Cab, he bought him a new piano—a baby grand he came by third hand—and he gave me the ole honky tonk. My daddy put it up in the kitchen, and I played it every chance I got; and it seemed like Slim was right there with me.

After that, it was me upstairs on the honky tonk and one piano player after another downstairs on the baby grand. They came from all over, but one thing's for sure—could they ever play! Stride and rag and jazz and blues and most anything else you could think of. There was even one of 'em—his name was Billy Gunn—who played with two fingers stuck straight out and his thumb held up like his hand was a revolver.

My daddy helped Cab fix up a little stage for the baby grand, and the Bird Nest turned itself into a night club. It wasn't just the neighborhood folks that came there any more, but rich folks and ladies in furs. I took it all in, keepin' outta sight behind the curtains and the lightin'. Cab always said if there was any kind of trouble, I was to slip out the side door into the garage, and fast!

The night Ray Slide was playin', there were lots of musicians in the place. Why, even Earl Golson, the famous sax man, was there! My momma used to play his records all the time.

NOT YET, BOSS. HE WAS IN TOO MUCH OF A HURRY TO START PLAYIN' IN SOME HOLE OVER ON THE OTHER SIDE OF TOWN!.

GO, MAKE SURE HE DOESN'T TALK. HE KNOWS TOO MUCH!

OK, BOSS, I'LL TAKE CARE OF HIM

GOT THE TOOLS, ALDO?

OKAY, ALDO, GO DO YOUR STUFF. I'LL COVER YOU.

RAT!
TAT!
TAT!
TAT!

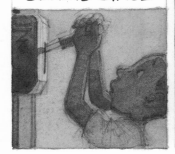

BEHIND STAGE

COME ON, RAY, WE GOTTA GET OUTTA HERE!

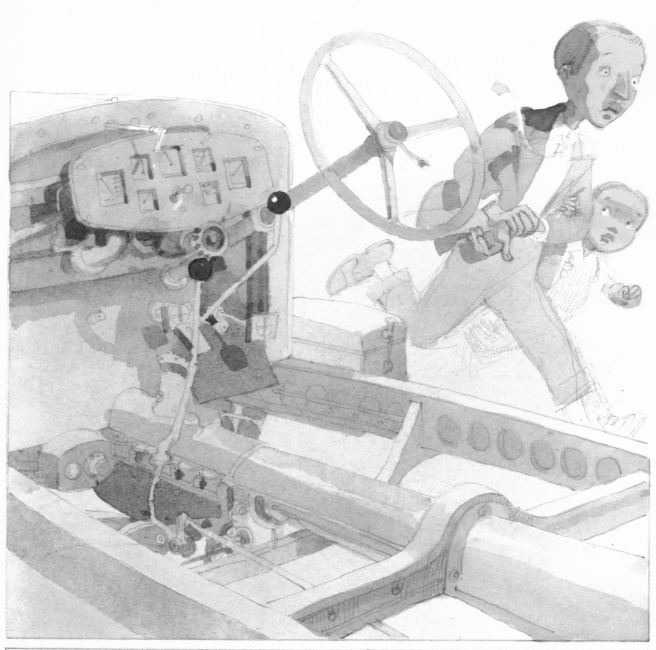

HEY! OVER HERE ... A DOOR...

... TO A GARAGE!

MAYBE IN ONE OF THOSE HEAPS.

HE'S GOTTA BE HERE! I'LL CHECK THE INSIDES, YOU GET THE TRUNKS!.

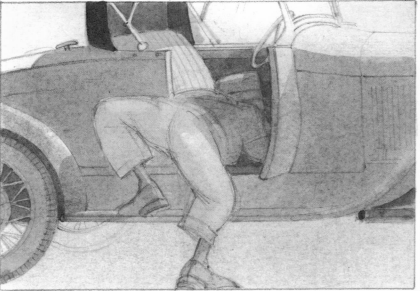

HE AIN'T HERE

WE WOULD'VE HEARD HIM IF HE'D OPENED THE GARAGE DOOR.

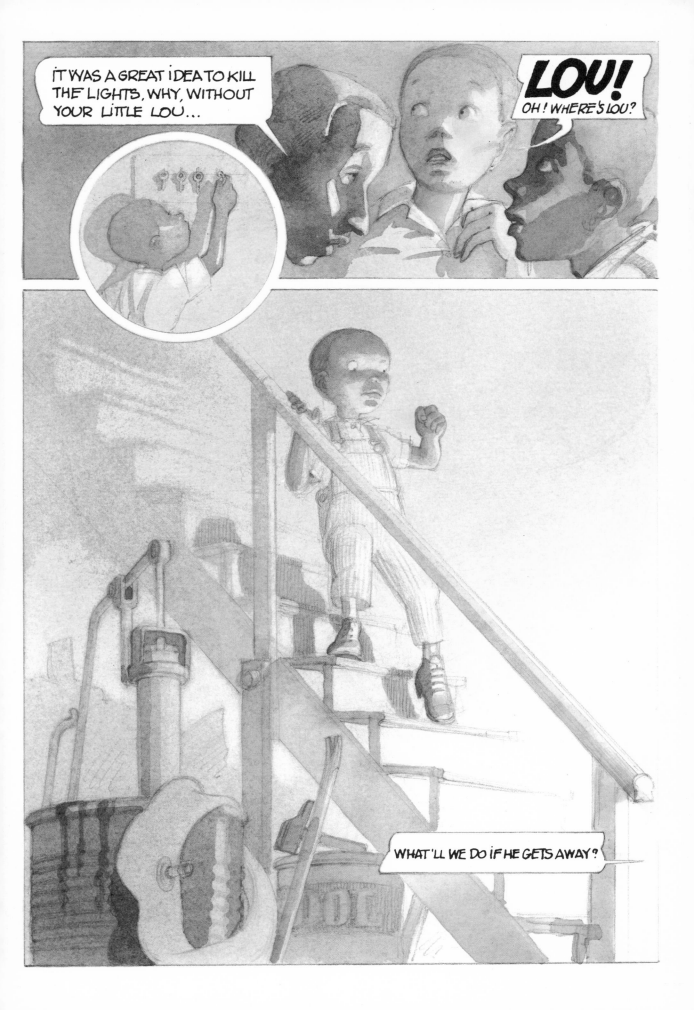

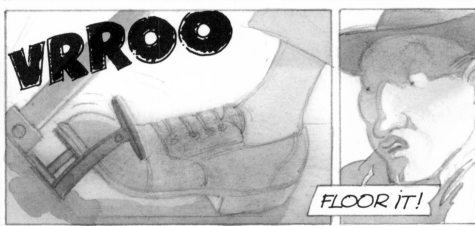

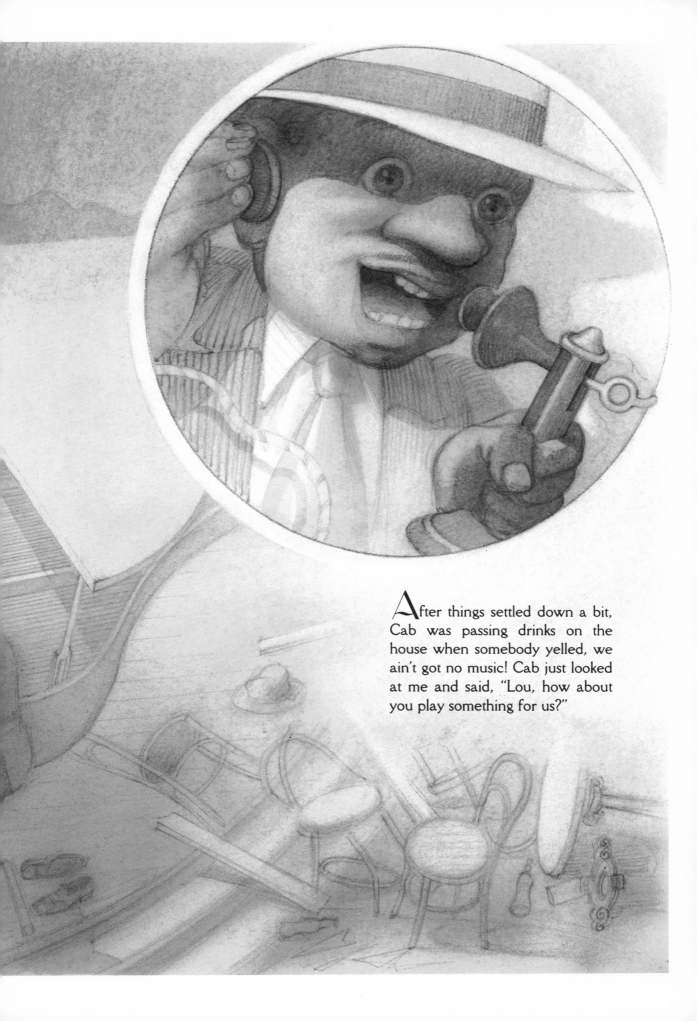

After things settled down a bit, Cab was passing drinks on the house when somebody yelled, we ain't got no music! Cab just looked at me and said, "Lou, how about you play something for us?"

Well, there I was, right in front of Earl Golson and Ray
Slide and some others I didn't even know. But I sat down at
that baby grand, and I played Tin Lizzie Rag, a tune Slim
had wrote for my daddy.

They loved it! Earl went and called for his sax . . .

And an hour later, I was playin' with a real live band.

Turned out that Ray was the reason Earl Golson came to the Bird Nest that night. He was lookin' for a piano player for his next concert.

Poor Ole Ray. The doc told him left hand only for the next three weeks.

So Ray sat down right next to me and kept me workin' right up to the day of the show.

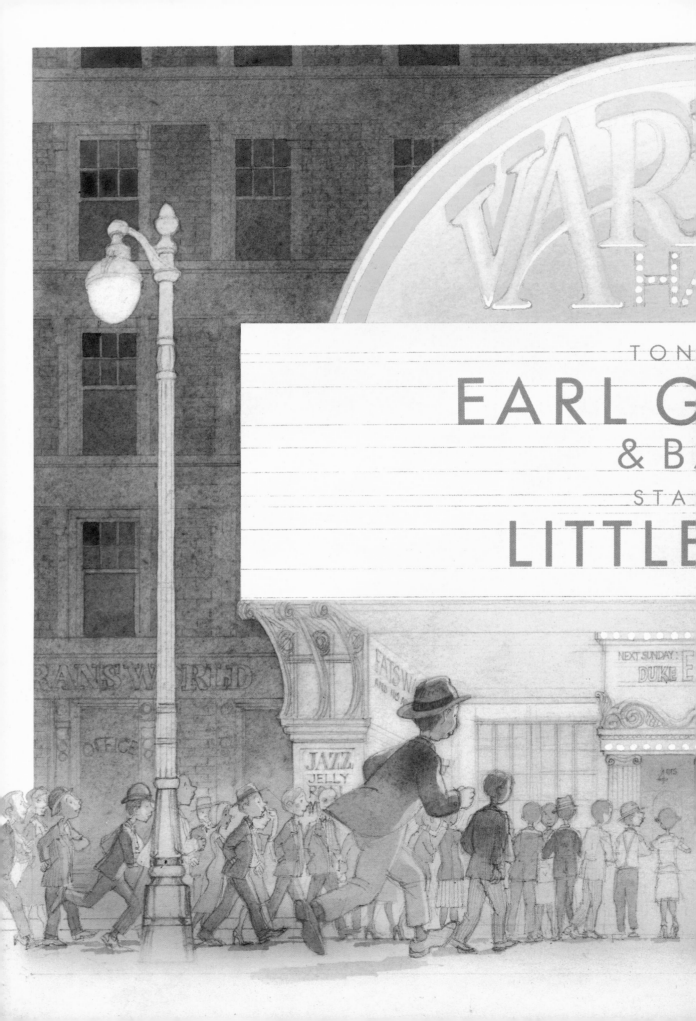

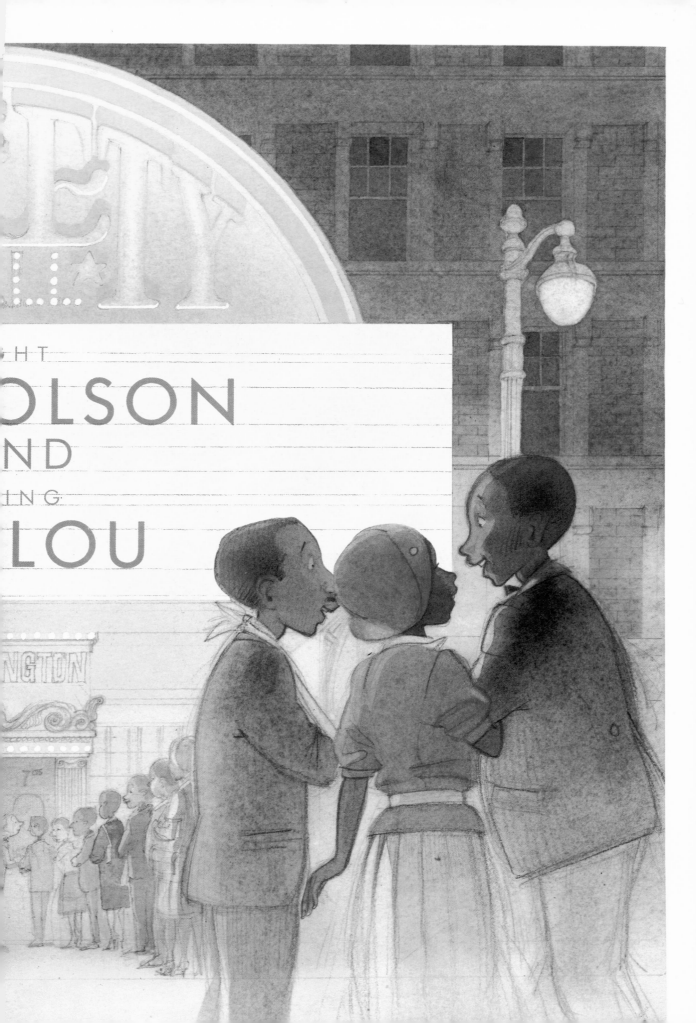